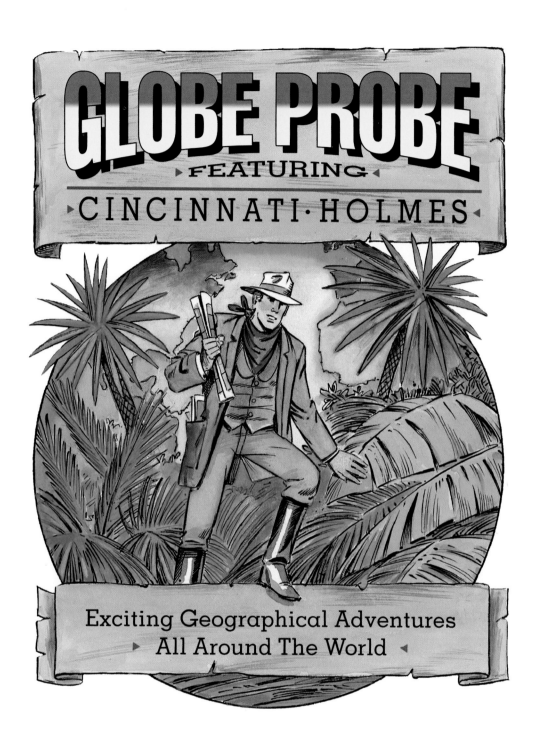

GLOBE PROBE
FEATURING
CINCINNATI · HOLMES

Exciting Geographical Adventures
▶ All Around The World ◀

From the journals of Dr. Croftsford Holmes

Edited by Jeffrey A. O'Hare
Illustrated by Carlos Garzon

BELL BOOKS
BOYDS MILLS PRESS

Published by Bell Books
Boyds Mills Press, Inc.
A Highlights Company
910 Church Street
Honesdale, Pennsylvania 18431

Publisher Cataloging-in-Publication Data
O'Hare, Jeffrey A.
Globe probe : featuring Cincinnati Holmes : exciting geographical
adventures all around the world : from the journals of Dr. Croftsford
Holmes / edited by Jeffrey A. O'Hare ; illustrated by Carlos Garzon.—1st ed.
[32] p. : col. ill. ; cm. + maps
Summary: The fictional adventurer and cartographer Cincinnati Holmes leads
readers on an exciting trip all around the globe. His discoveries about
geography offer readers information about social studies, geography, and map
skills. Riddles, puzzles, and games supplement the text.
ISBN 1-56397-037-6
1. Maps—Juvenile literature. 2. Scientific recreations—Juvenile literature.
[1. Maps. 2. Scientific recreations.] I. Garzon, Carlos, ill. II. Title.
912—dc20   1993
Library of Congress Catalog Card Number: 91-77619

First edition, 1993
Book designed by Charlie Cary
The text of this book is set in 12-point Times Ten.
The illustrations are done in ink and watercolor.

Distributed by St. Martin's Press

Printed in Mexico
Reinforced trade edition

10 9 8 7 6 5 4 3 2 1

INTRODUCTION

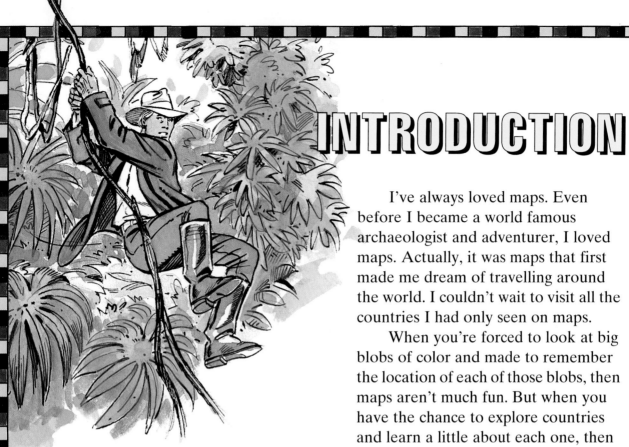

Shalom! Benvenuto! Hola! Bon Jour! Strasvitziya! Guten Tag! Nihow! Parev!

These are all ways to say "Hello!" in some of the world's many different languages. When you travel, you learn a lot of fascinating customs, meet interesting people, and see some amazing sites. Everything from ancient civilizations to modern cities can be yours. Though you might not be able to afford the airfare, you can still journey to exotic locations and faraway places just by looking at a map.

Maps are wondrous things. With just a touch of imagination, they can show you countries, oceans, and islands. You can use maps to climb majestic mountains and paddle down raging rivers. And you never even have to leave the comfort of your own bedroom.

I've always loved maps. Even before I became a world famous archaeologist and adventurer, I loved maps. Actually, it was maps that first made me dream of travelling around the world. I couldn't wait to visit all the countries I had only seen on maps.

When you're forced to look at big blobs of color and made to remember the location of each of those blobs, then maps aren't much fun. But when you have the chance to explore countries and learn a little about each one, then there's excitement, danger, maybe even a bit of romance.

In this book, I've put together some of my favorite map adventures. There are puzzles, quizzes, games, and a world of interesting information. But don't worry. If any of these adventures prove to be too tough, I've even included the answers in the back. Best of all, there's even a terrific map for you to examine and enjoy.

After reading through this journal, I hope that you too will discover the excitement in maps. I'll look for you as I continue to probe every part of our fascinating globe.

Your friend,

Croftsford Holmes

Croftsford "Cincinnati" Holmes
Professor of Archaeology & Cartography
Miskatonic University

AFRICA

Africa is the second largest continent. The largest African country, Sudan, is bigger than Alaska and Texas combined. The smallest, an island country called the Seychelles, is only about half the size of the city of New Orleans, Louisiana.

Africa produces most of the world's cashews, cocoa leaves, cassava, and yams.

It has tremendous mineral wealth in the form of copper, gold, diamonds, and petroleum. There are natural rivers and waterfalls that can be harnessed to produce vast amounts of hydroelectric power. Also there are valuable forests, but so far Africa has the least developed economy of any continent except Antarctica.

Oil is one of Africa's major exports, most of it coming

GEO FACTS

Highest point: Mount Kilimanjaro in Tanzania (19,341 feet)

Lowest point: Shores of Lake Assal in Djibouti (508 feet below sea level)

Longest river: Nile in Egypt, Sudan, and other countries (4,160 miles)

Largest lake: Lake Victoria in Uganda, Tanzania, and other countries (26,828 square miles)

from western countries like Nigeria.

Soccer is a very popular spectator sport in Africa. Soccer stadiums can be found in almost every major city throughout the continent.

Africa lies on both the equator, which is O° latitude, and on the Prime Meridian, which is O° longitude. Therefore, it is the only continent with some land

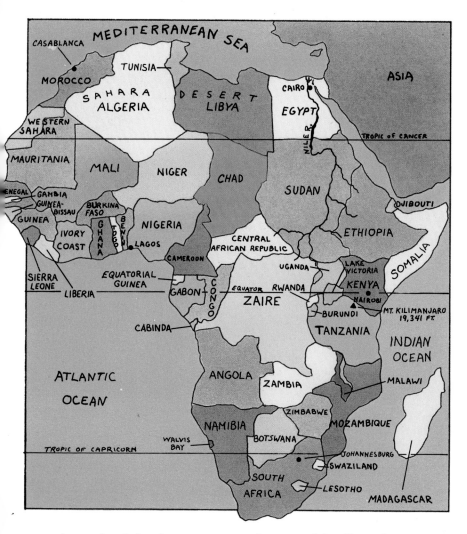

MAJOR CITIES

Casablanca, Morocco

Nairobi, Kenya

Cairo, Egypt

Lagos, Nigeria

Johannesburg, South Africa

area, some countries like Ethiopia are experiencing severe famine.

Nigeria has the largest population in Africa, with over 118 million people. This number is made up of more than 250 tribes, including the Hausa, the Yoruba, and the Ibo.

Another major African tribe is the Masai, who are cattle herders of the Serengeti. Other herding tribes include the Dinka, Fulani, and the Turkana.

Family is of great importance in African life. A family home is usually extended to include grandparents, uncles, aunts, and cousins.

Africa has a rich tradition of oral literature, which is the passing of stories from one generation to another. These stories are sometimes chanted to music, and used in religious ceremonies. They are used to pass along values and traditions.

mass in each of the four hemispheres.

If you look around the coast of Africa, you will see no major indentations of the land mass. This means there aren't any good natural harbors. But man has built many great ports along the

rivers and bodies of water that surround the continent.

The northern third of Africa is mainly desert, while the central third is taken up by lush rain forest.

Egypt is the site of many wonders, including the ancient pyramids and the Great Sphinx. From modern times, it is also the home of the Aswan High Dam, a major irrigation project on the Nile River.

Even though the Nile River forms a rich agricultural

GEO FEATURES

Nile River

Sahara Desert

Victoria Falls

NAME THE GAME

I'm looking on the map for the names of some of my friends. Each friend lives in a country whose name contains their name. For instance, my friend Tina can be found in Argentina. Can you find at least one country for all my other friends?

ADA _____

AL _____

ANA _____

ARI _____

BEN _____

CHAD _____

DOMINIC _____

DON _____

FRAN _____

GARY _____

GERI _____

GUY _____

IRA _____

KEN _____

LEON _____

LIZ _____

MAL _____

MARK _____

PHILIP _____

SAL _____

STAN _____

TRINI _____

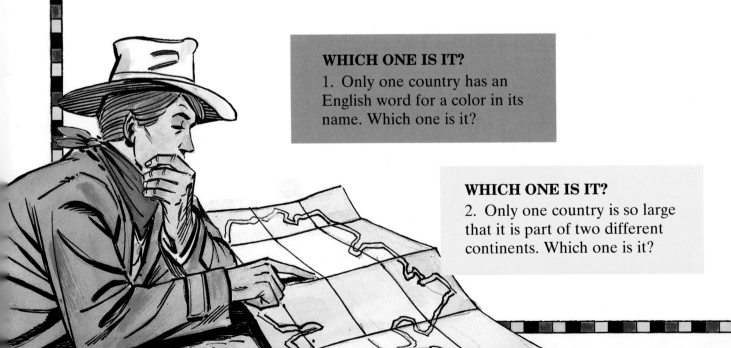

WHICH ONE IS IT?
1. Only one country has an English word for a color in its name. Which one is it?

WHICH ONE IS IT?
2. Only one country is so large that it is part of two different continents. Which one is it?

CAPITAL LETTERS

The last time I let my valuable archaeological collection go on tour, the exhibit went to museums around the world. The collection was scheduled to stop at eleven world capitals, but somehow the route got all mixed up. Can you unscramble the name of each capital, and then help me find the countries on my map?

When the names are unscrambled, look at the number on each line. That is the number letter you are looking for in that row. For example, the first line has a 4. Find the fourth letter in the unscrambled capital. If you locate each letter correctly, you should spell out the eleventh country the tour visited. Hint: This country's capital is Belgrade.

KOTOY, Japan _____ 4

STERACHUB, Romania _____ 2

GALSO, Nigeria _____ 3

GONNAY, Myanmar _____ 5

SERUMEJAL, Israel _____ 5

DONNOL, England _____ 1

RABERANC, Australia _____ 8

TENVIDEOMO, Uruguay _____ 6

IPETIA, Taiwan _____ 3

NOHIA, Vietnam _____ 2

ANTARCTICA

Antarctica is the fifth largest continent. No other continent is as cold, harsh, or desolate. The ground and surrounding seas are almost always frozen solid. All the supplies needed by scientists have to be brought in by ship during the summer months of November to January. During these months, the ice is thin enough to allow icebreakers through to reach the land.

Antarctica can be translated as "Opposite the Bear." The Bear refers to Ursa Major, the northern constellation which appears above the Arctic Ocean.

The Arctic, which is at the North Pole, is not really a continent at all. Actually it is an ocean, which is frozen throughout the winter.

The world's record coldest temperature (-128.6° F) was recorded in 1983 at Russia's Vostok Base, which is approximately 800 miles from the South Pole.

No one lives permanently in Antarctica because it is so cold and desolate. A number of research stations have been set up on Antarctica. These are used by rotating shifts of scientists. Among the many experiments being carried on here is the ongoing measurement of the atmosphere's ozone layer.

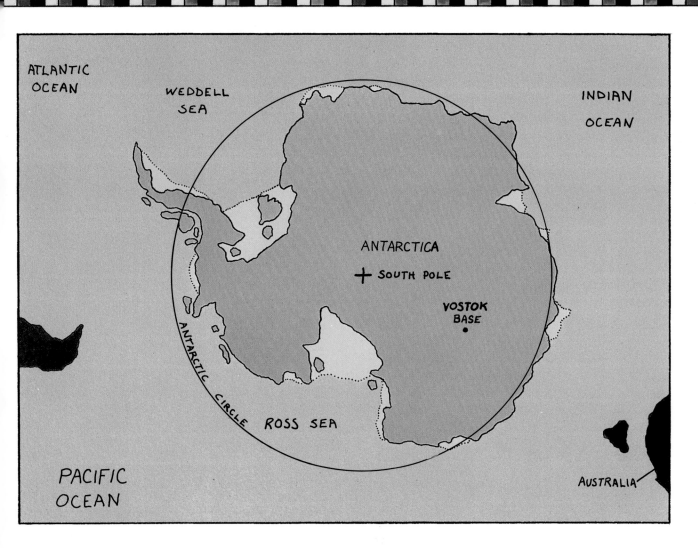

ATLANTIC OCEAN

WEDDELL SEA

INDIAN OCEAN

ANTARCTICA

✛ SOUTH POLE

VOSTOK BASE

ANTARCTIC CIRCLE

ROSS SEA

PACIFIC OCEAN

AUSTRALIA

No land animals can exist here either, but there are plenty of penguins, seals, and whales.

No single country has a claim on this continent. Argentina, Australia, Chile, France, Great Britain, New Zealand, and Norway all lay claim to some part of this continent. The United States and Russia also operate research facilities on Antarctica.

PICTURE PERFECT

When I travel, I often draw pictures of the places I visit. That way I'll always have a souvenir of the trip. Unfortunately, when I was putting these pictures in my album, the labels blew off. Now I don't remember which country is represented in each scene. Help me arrange these pictures by labeling them with the proper country.

2. _____

1. _____

3. _____

4. _____

5. _____

6. _____

7. _____

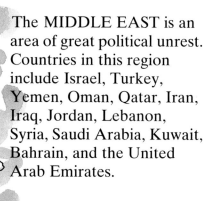

ASIA

The MIDDLE EAST is an area of great political unrest. Countries in this region include Israel, Turkey, Yemen, Oman, Qatar, Iran, Iraq, Jordan, Lebanon, Syria, Saudi Arabia, Kuwait, Bahrain, and the United Arab Emirates.

SOUTH ASIA is where you'll find India, Pakistan, Afghanistan, Bangladesh, Nepal, and Sri Lanka.

SOUTHEAST ASIA is an area that most people are familiar with. Among the countries in this region are

Geo Facts

Highest point: Mount Everest in Tibet is the world's tallest mountain at 29,028 feet.

Lowest point: The shores of the Dead Sea in Israel and Jordan are at 1,312 feet below sea level.

Longest river: The Yenisei in Russia measures in at 3,442 miles, while the Yangtze in China is right behind at 3,437 miles.

Vietnam, Laos, Cambodia, Thailand, Myanmar, Brunei, Philippines, Malaysia, and Indonesia.

The FAR EAST region includes mainland China, Singapore, Mongolia, North Korea, South Korea, and Taiwan.

Other notable areas of Asia include Japan and parts of Russia. Russia is so big, it is actually part of two different continents.

Governments in Asia range from the absolute monarchies

Asia is the largest of all seven continents. It boasts both the highest and lowest land points in the world. Approximately 30% of the world's land area is in Asia. Asia also has the biggest population. The countries of China, India, and the Russian Republics have a combined total of more than two billion people.

Asia is one of the more geographically diverse continents. It is divided into many distinct areas.

Geo Features

The Persian Gulf

The Arabian Peninsula

The Himalayan Mountains

Lake Baikal

Red Sea

Dead Sea

Yangtze River

Mekong River

in Oman to military regimes like the one in Myanmar to democratic governments, as in India.

Asia is home to the largest variety of religions. Hindus make up 20% of the total population. Buddhism, Judaism, Christianity, Islam, and Confucianism are among the major religions, along with Shintoism, Taoism, Sikhism, and Zoroastrianism.

One major city, Hong Kong, is almost a country unto itself. By way of treaty, Hong Kong is currently a

British protectorate, but at the end of the 20th century it will return to being governed by China.

Major Cities of Asia

Beijing, China

Tokyo, Japan

Kyoto, Japan

Hong Kong

Bangkok, Thailand

Jerusalem, Israel

Mecca, Saudi Arabia

Bombay, India

Asia has been the site of many major conflicts, such as the Korean War and the Vietnam War.

Animals that are native to Asia include the Indian elephant, Indian rhinoceros, Bengal tiger, Komodo dragon, crocodile, snow leopard, reindeer, camel, yak, tapir, mongoose, and of course, China's giant panda.

Important products that come from Asia include tea, wool, fish, rice, gemstones, and oil.

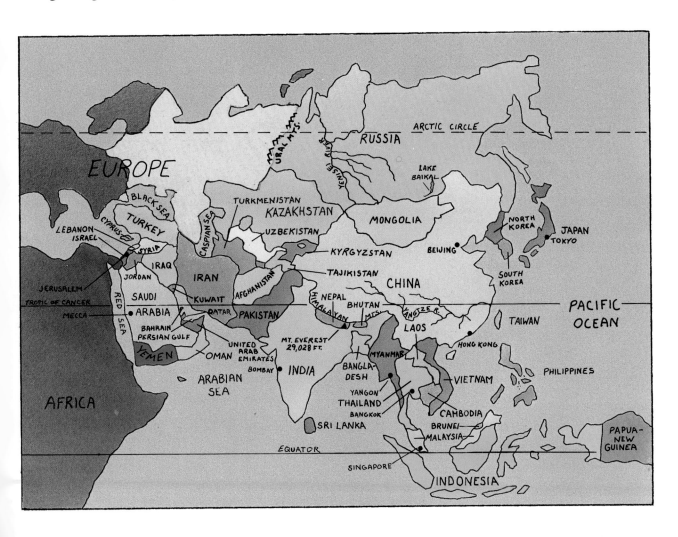

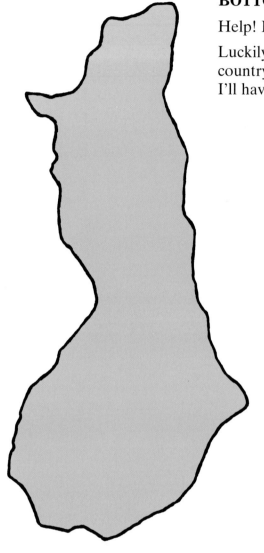

BOTTOM TO TOP

Help! I can't remember the name of the country pictured here.

Luckily, I know a way to figure out the name of this particular country. If I can match each capital city below with its country, I'll have my first set of clues.

Copenhagen _____

Katmandu _____

Buenos Aires _____

Tripoli _____

Wellington _____

Rome _____

Paris _____

Now reading the first letter of each country, going from bottom to top, will reveal the name of the pictured country. Can you find it on my map?

WHICH ONE IS IT?
4. There is only one letter in the alphabet that does not appear as the first letter in the name of any country. Which letter is it?

FLAG FUN

As a world famous adventurer, I've been almost everywhere. I've seen so many national flags that I sometimes get them mixed up. On this page are some of my favorite flags. Next to each is a picture of the country it represents. Find each country on my map and then write the name under each flag to help me remember.

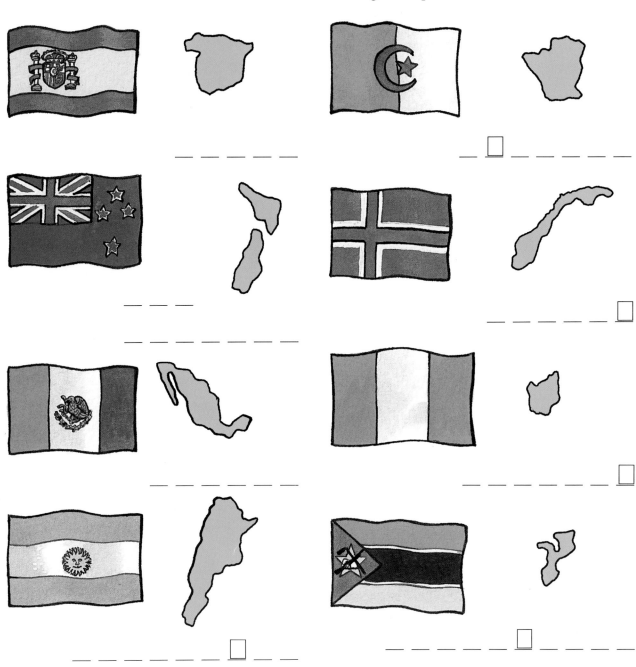

If you unscramble the boxed letters, you will find the name of the only country whose flag contains only one color.

AUSTRALIA

Australia is the world's largest island, but it is also the smallest continent.

Ayers Rock, in the heart of central Australia's desert, is the largest monolith on Earth. A monolith is a solid, large single stone. Ayers Rock is more than two miles long, 1,100 feet high, and five and a half miles around.

Australia has some of the world's most unique animals. The duck-billed platypus, the snake-necked tortoise, the hairy-nosed

wombat, the greater bilby, the wallaby, and the kangaroo are some animals that are found only in Australia.

The earliest known inhabitants of Australia are the Aborigines. Before the coming of Europeans, Aborigines were nomadic hunters who lived a mostly peaceful existence. There are almost 500 different tribes of Aborigines, and each tribe has its own unique language. Kangaroo and koala are just

two of the many words that have come into the English language from the Aborigines.

Australia is the world's largest producer of wool. Minerals such as copper, iron ore, coal, and bauxite are also plentiful here.

Though Australia is an independent country, it is a member of the British Commonwealth. This means that although Australia has

Geo Facts

Highest point: Mount Kosciusko at 7,310 feet.

Lowest point: Lake Eyre, which is 52 feet below sea level.

Largest Lake: Lake Eyre at 3,700 square miles.

Longest river: the Murray-Darling, which runs over 2,330 miles.

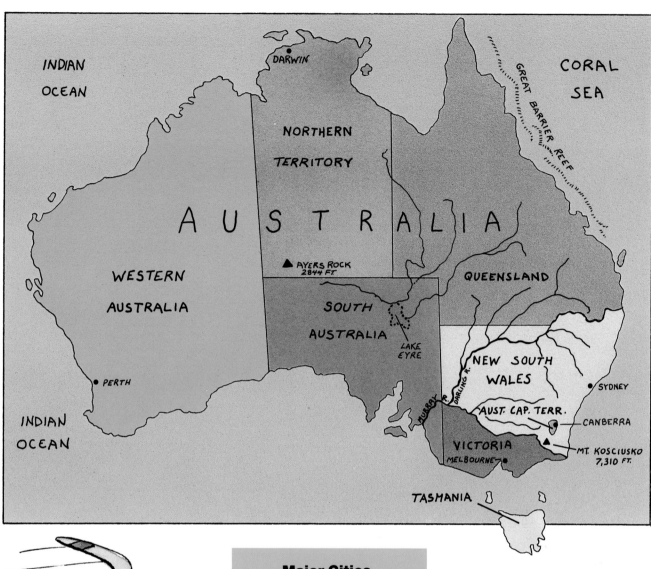

INDIAN OCEAN

DARWIN

NORTHERN TERRITORY

CORAL SEA

GREAT BARRIER REEF

AUSTRALIA

WESTERN AUSTRALIA

▲ AYERS ROCK 2844 FT.

QUEENSLAND

SOUTH AUSTRALIA

LAKE EYRE

• PERTH

INDIAN OCEAN

NEW SOUTH WALES

• SYDNEY

MURRAY R.

DARLING R.

AUST. CAP. TERR.

CANBERRA

VICTORIA

MELBOURNE •

▲ MT. KOSCIUSKO 7,310 FT.

TASMANIA

its own laws and government, it is united with other nations for purposes of mutual assistance. Canada and New Zealand are other commonwealth nations.

Geo Features

Ayers Rock

The Great Barrier Reef

Major Cities

Canberra

Darwin

Melbourne

Perth

Sydney

Other major land areas in this part of the world include Fiji, New Zealand, Papua-New Guinea, and Tasmania, an island that is part of Australia.

One of the world's favorite toys came from the outback of Australia. The boomerang is used by Aborigines while hunting. Though treated as a toy in the United States, a boomerang can be very deadly when handled by an experienced hunter.

Australians have a game called Australian Rules Football. It is different from American football or any other game. Cricket, a baseball-like game brought over from England, is very popular, as is soccer.

THE BIGGEST AND THE BEST

This list contains some of the most impressive sights I've seen in my travels. I'll give you a description and the area where each feature is located. See if you can come up with its name.

1. The tallest mountain in the world is located in Nepal. _____

2. The longest river is located in Africa. _____

3. The second largest country in square miles is in North America. _____

4. The most populous country is in Asia. _____

5. The longest mountain range is found in South America. _____

6. The world's largest ocean is between the Americas and Asia. _____

7. The largest desert is in northern Africa. _____

8. The highest waterfall is in Venezuela. _____

9. The world's lowest point is located in the Middle East. _____

10. The largest lake in the world is located in Iran and Russia. It's called the Caspian Sea and is 143,630 square miles. The second largest lake is in the United States. Which one is it?

_____

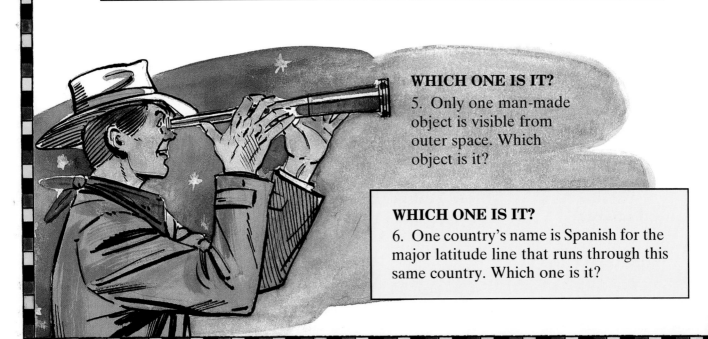

WHICH ONE IS IT?
5. Only one man-made object is visible from outer space. Which object is it?

WHICH ONE IS IT?
6. One country's name is Spanish for the major latitude line that runs through this same country. Which one is it?

WHAT WAS THAT NAME AGAIN?

I once hired a guide while travelling. Sherpa was the guide's name and he was very nice, but there was one problem. Whenever I showed Sherpa a country I wanted to visit, he could only remember the country by a former name. For instance, he only knew the country of Sri Lanka by its former name, which was Ceylon.

See if you can guide me through this mess by identifying each country below. The countries are pictured here as shown on my map. Beside each country is one name that it was known by in the past. Please find each country on the map and write its current name on the line next to it.

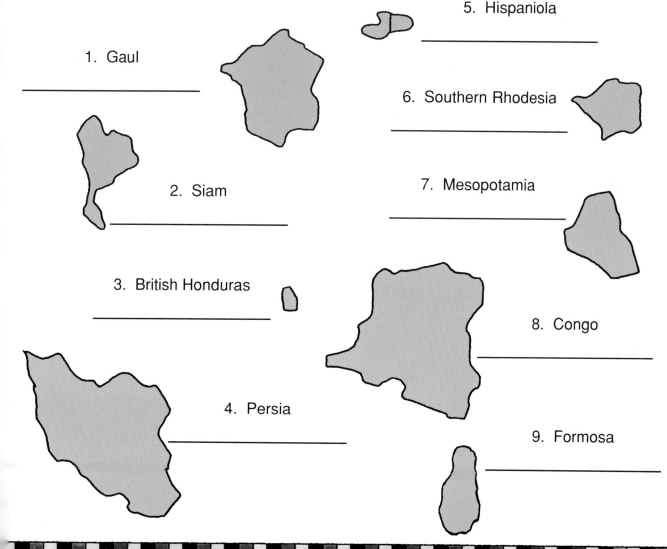

5. Hispaniola
_____

1. Gaul
_____

6. Southern Rhodesia
_____

2. Siam
_____

7. Mesopotamia
_____

3. British Honduras
_____

8. Congo
_____

4. Persia
_____

9. Formosa
_____

EUROPE

For easy identification, Europe can be divided into major geographical areas:

The BRITISH ISLES include Ireland, Northern Ireland, England, Scotland, and Wales.

BENELUX countries are BElgium, NEtherlands, and LUXembourg. The name came from the first few letters of each country.

Geo Features

The Alps, a set of mountains in Italy and Switzerland

Danube, a river located in Germany, Austria, and other countries

English Channel, a body of water between England and France

Loch Ness, a small body of water in Scotland

The Balkan Peninsula

The Carpathians, mountains found in Romania

The Eiffel Tower, Paris, France

These countries formed an economic union following World War II. Though they are grouped together, each maintains its own form of government.

SCANDINAVIA is in northern Europe. There is no single country called Scandinavia. The countries in this region are Iceland, Norway, Denmark, Sweden, and Finland.

EASTERN EUROPE includes the countries of Poland, Czechoslovakia, Hungary, Romania, Armenia, Azerbaijan, Georgia, Ukraine, Moldava, Bulgaria, Belarus, and Russia.

Famous landmarks in Europe include Buckingham Palace in England, the Louvre and the Eiffel Tower in France, the Colosseum in Italy, and the Parthenon in Greece.

A tunnel was built below the English Channel. This tunnel allows both trains and automobiles to travel between England and France.

From the end of World War II until 1990, Germany was actually two separate countries, divided into East and West. There were two separate capitals and two separate governments.

Two European cultures use alphabets that are different from the Roman alphabet used by most English-speaking countries. Russia uses the Cyrillic alphabet, which is based on both Latin and Greek letters. Greece uses an alphabet like the one below:

αγαπάμε τους χάρτες

Major Cities

London, England

Paris, France

Rome, Italy

Madrid, Spain

Moscow, Russia

Dublin, Ireland

Belfast, Northern Ireland

People don't usually think of wild animals when they think of Europe. Yet wildlife is abundant throughout the continent. The ibex, wolf, tortoise, squirrel, reindeer, bear, wild boar, lynx, fox, European bison, and wolverine are some of the animals found in Europe.

Both World War I and World War II were fought primarily on European soil.

Europe is smaller than every other continent except Australia, yet only Asia has more people.

There are many small countries which are part of Europe. These include Andorra at 180 square miles, Malta at 122 square miles, San Marino at 23.4 square miles, Monaco at .65 square miles, and Vatican City at .17 square miles.

Geo Facts

Highest point in all Europe: Mount Elbrus in southern Russia (18,481 feet). Excluding all the former members of the Soviet Union, the highest European point is Mount Blanc (15,771 feet), which is located on the border between France and Italy.

Lowest land point: Some parts of the Netherlands are below sea level.

Longest river: The Volga in Russia (2,293 miles)

Largest lake: The Caspian Sea (143,630 square miles). Parts of the Caspian Sea are located in Asia.

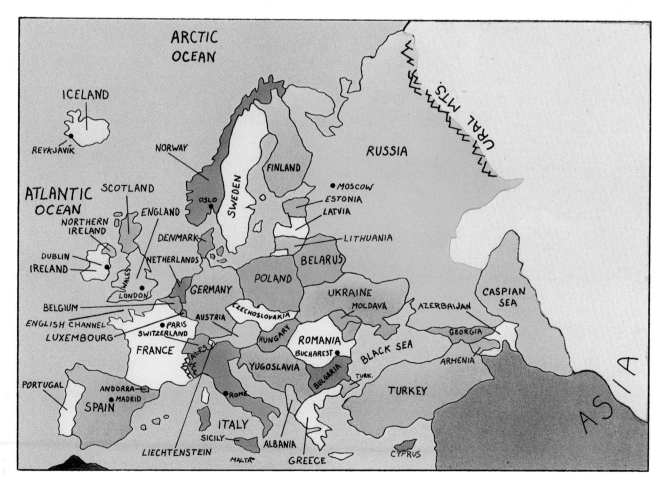

ENDANGERED ANIMALS

As an adventurer, I've been lucky enough to get into the wild to see many of the animals that are facing extinction. I like to take pictures of these animals so I can show others the beauty we will lose if these creatures die out. On this page are some of the pictures I've taken, along with a drawing of the country where each animal was found. Can you unscramble the name of each country to discover where a few of these animals can still be found in the wild?

YANEK

RAIZE

ANIDI

PLANE

NAZNATIA

NICHA

LIZARB

ALARUSTIA

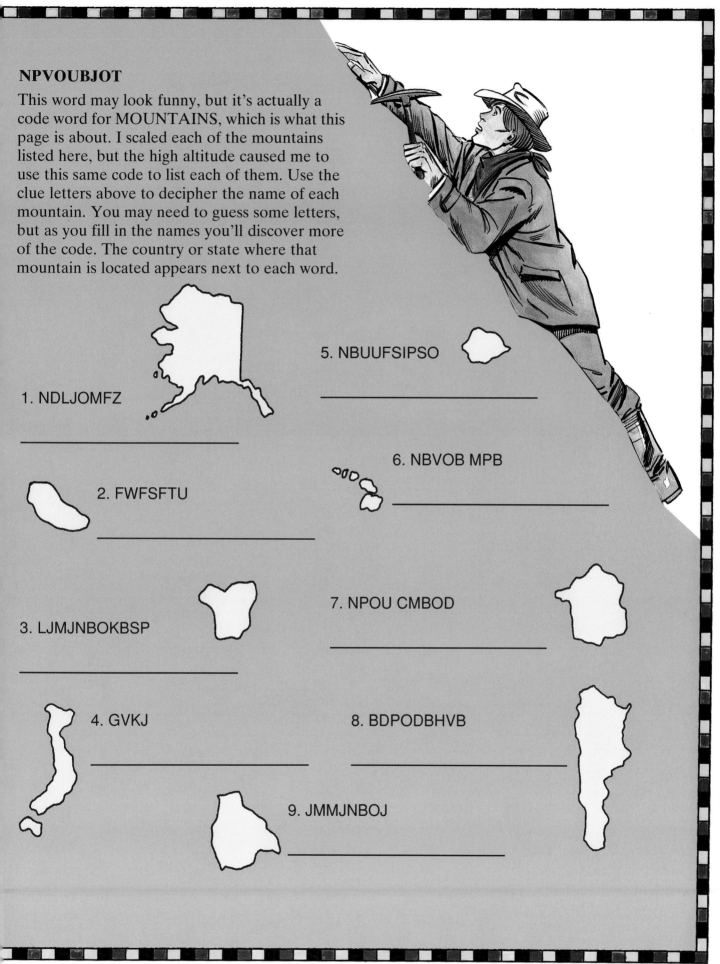

NPVOUBJOT

This word may look funny, but it's actually a code word for MOUNTAINS, which is what this page is about. I scaled each of the mountains listed here, but the high altitude caused me to use this same code to list each of them. Use the clue letters above to decipher the name of each mountain. You may need to guess some letters, but as you fill in the names you'll discover more of the code. The country or state where that mountain is located appears next to each word.

1. NDLJOMFZ

_____

2. FWFSFTU

_____

3. LJMJNBOKBSP

_____

4. GVKJ

_____

5. NBUUFSIPSO

_____

6. NBVOB MPB

_____

7. NPOU CMBOD

_____

8. BDPODBHVB

_____

9. JMMJNBOJ

_____

NORTH AMERICA

Canada and the United States, two of the largest countries in the world, are included on this continent.

CANADA is the second largest country in the world, yet it is not heavily populated. There are two territories and ten provinces that make up Canada. These are the Yukon Territory, the Northwest Territories, British Columbia, Saskatchewan, Quebec, Manitoba, Ontario, Nova Scotia, Newfoundland, Alberta, New Brunswick, and Prince Edward Island.

The U.S. has more cars on the road than any other country.

The UNITED STATES OF AMERICA is perhaps the richest country in the world when it comes to natural resources. There is prairie land that can supply wheat, corn, soybeans, potatoes, and other crops. Abundant forests provide timber and paper. Oil can be found in certain areas. There are mountains, seashores, lakes, and rivers.

Yet all these resources may be in danger if not managed properly. Wildlife management, conservation, replanting, and recycling are all ways people can help make the most of the resources they have.

GREENLAND is a large island north of Canada. Formerly, it was a colony of Denmark.

CENTRAL AMERICA is made up of eight countries.

Geo Facts

Highest point: Mount McKinley in Alaska at 20,320 feet.

Lowest point: Death Valley, California, at 282 feet below sea level.

Longest river: The Mississippi at 3,710 miles.

Largest lake: Lake Superior at 31,795 square miles.

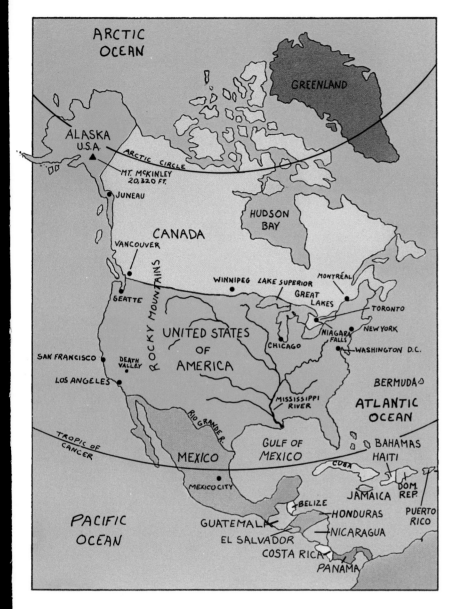

ARCTIC OCEAN

GREENLAND

ALASKA U.S.A.

ARCTIC CIRCLE

MT. McKINLEY 20,320 FT.

JUNEAU

HUDSON BAY

CANADA

VANCOUVER

WINNIPEG   LAKE SUPERIOR

GREAT LAKES

MONTREAL

SEATTLE

ROCKY MOUNTAINS

UNITED STATES OF AMERICA

CHICAGO

TORONTO

NIAGARA FALLS

NEW YORK

WASHINGTON D.C.

SAN FRANCISCO

DEATH VALLEY

LOS ANGELES

BERMUDA

ATLANTIC OCEAN

MISSISSIPPI RIVER

TROPIC OF CANCER

RIO GRANDE R.

MEXICO

GULF OF MEXICO

BAHAMAS

HAITI

CUBA

MEXICO CITY

JAMAICA

DOM. REP.

PUERTO RICO

PACIFIC OCEAN

GUATEMALA

EL SALVADOR

BELIZE

HONDURAS

NICARAGUA

COSTA RICA

PANAMA

Major Cities

Vancouver, British Columbia

Montreal, Quebec

Toronto, Ontario

Washington, D.C.

New York, New York

Los Angeles, California

San Francisco, California

Chicago, Illinois

Mexico City, Mexico

Geo Features

Niagara Falls

The Grand Canyon

Rocky Mountains

Rio Grande River

Gulf of Mexico

The Great Lakes

A trick for remembering the names of the Great Lakes is to think of the word HOMES. That stands for Huron, Ontario, Michigan, Erie, and Superior, which are the names of the lakes.

These are Belize, Guatemala, El Salvador, Nicaragua, Costa Rica, Panama, Honduras, and Mexico. Six of these countries have coasts on two sides.

A number of smaller islands are also in this area. Farming used to be the top industry of this region, but tourism has since become more important.

Magnificent mountain ranges mark this continent. Such ranges include the Rockies in the west and the Appalachians in the east.

THE CARIBBEAN ISLANDS are sometimes known as the West Indies. These include Cuba, Haiti, the Dominican Republic, Jamaica, Barbados, the Bahamas, and Puerto Rico.

WHICH ONE IS IT?

7. The name of one European country contains the full name of the capital city of a different European country. The capital's name appears in order and is not scrambled. Which country and which capital are they?

WHERE ARE THEY?

Use the map to see if you can answer these questions and solve the riddle below.

1. Which country is farther south?
   If Argentina, put a C in spaces 3 and 20.
   If Australia, put a C in spaces 3 and 24.
2. What country lies at 0° latitude (the equator)?
   If Germany, put a T in spaces 9, 22 and 28.
   If Gabon, put a T in spaces 10 and 24.
3. If Alaska is part of the United States, put an R in space 27.
   If Alaska is part of Canada, put an R in spaces 15 and 18.
4. If Japan is east of China, put an N in space 15.
   If India is east of China, put an N in space 20.
5. If Madagascar is part of Asia, put a U in space 8.
   If Madagascar is part of Africa, put a U in space 5.
6. Greenland lies on an important line of latitude.
   If it is the Tropic of Cancer, put an O in spaces 19 and 23.
   If it is the Arctic Circle, put an O in space 8.
7. If Bangladesh is larger than Sweden, put a D in space 1.
   If Sweden is larger than Bangladesh, put a D in space 16.
8. If the Tropic of Capricorn is farther south, put a W in space 17.
   If the Tropic of Cancer is farther south, put a W in spaces 10 and 17.
9. If Bermuda is west of the United States, put a G in space 21.
   If Bermuda is east of the United States, put a B in space 1.
10. If Sierra Leone is a country in Africa, put an F in space 9.
    If Sierra Leone is a country in Latin America, put a Y in space 16.
11. If Italy is in the shape of a glove, put an I in space 8.
    If Italy is in the shape of a boot, put an I in spaces 19 and 22.
12. If any of Russia is south of the equator, put an H only in space 25.
    If all of Russia is north of the equator, put an H in spaces 11, 18, 21, and 25.
13. If Mexico is farther north than Venezuela, put an E in spaces 2, 7, 12, 26, and 28.
    If Venezuela is farther north, put a Q in spaces 2, 10 and 17.
14. If Cabinda is on Africa's west coast, put an A in spaces 4 and 14.
    If Cabinda is on Africa's east coast, put a J in spaces 3, 21 and 26.
15. If Pakistan is farther east than Turkey, put an S in spaces 6, 13 and 23.
    If Turkey is farther east than Pakistan, put an X in spaces 10 and 23.

Why do I never go hungry when I'm travelling through the desert?

__	__	__	__	__	__	__	__	__	__	__	__	__	__	__	__
1	2	3	4	5	6	7	8	9	10	11	12	13	14	15	16

__	__	__	__	__	__	__	__	__	__	__	__
17	18	19	20	21	22	23	24	25	26	27	28

ISLAND HOPPING

When people say they're going to the islands, that usually means they're going on a vacation. But when I go to the islands, I go exploring. To discover some of the islands I might visit, see if you can identify each of these island countries.

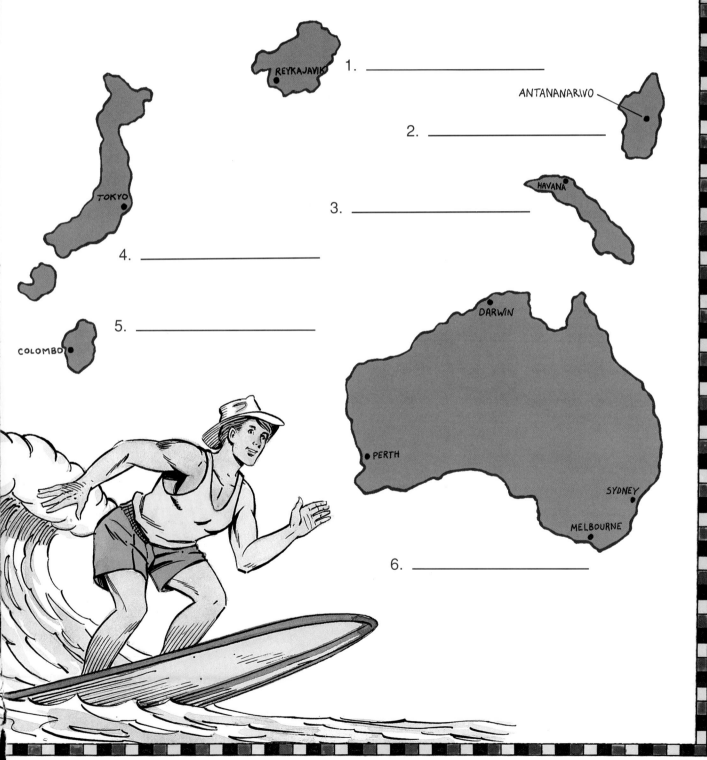

1. _____

2. _____

3. _____

4. _____

5. _____

6. _____

SOUTH AMERICA

South America is the fourth largest continent. Almost half of it is wilderness, made up of high mountains, empty plains, and tropical forests.

Brazil is the largest country in South America, taking up almost half the continent. The other countries in order of size (from largest to smallest) are Argentina, Peru, Colombia, Bolivia, Venezuela, Chile, Paraguay, Ecuador, Guyana, Uruguay, Suriname, and French Guiana.

On the Amazon River

Almost one-quarter of all known animal species in the world live in South America.

The largest number of these are found in the rain forests, plateaus, and swamps of the Amazon Basin. The biggest animal on the continent is the tapir, which can grow to be as large as a horse. Other uniquely South American animals are the llama, curassow, boa constrictor, yapok, coypu rat, alpaca, and the black caiman. The rain forest is one of

Geo Features

Angel Falls

Andes Mountains

Pampas Grassland

The Amazon River

and Rain forest

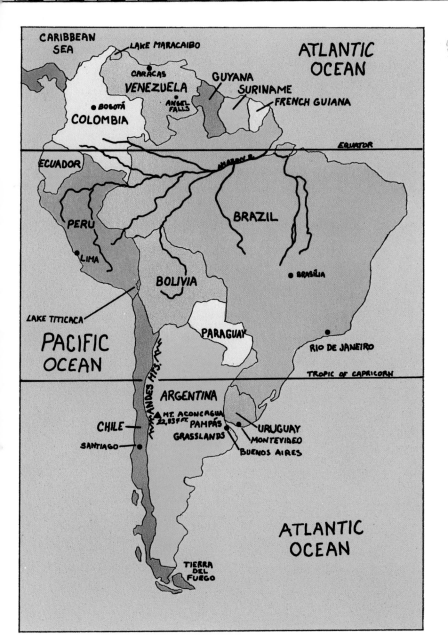

Geo Facts

Highest point: Mount Aconcagua in Argentina at 22,834 feet.

Lowest point: The Salinas Grande section of Argentina's Peninsula Valdes at 131 feet below sea level.

Longest river: Amazon in Brazil at 4,006 miles.

Largest lake: Lake Maracaibo in Venezuela covers more than 6,300 square miles.

Lake Titicaca in Bolivia and Peru, at 3,200 square miles, is the highest body of water in the world on which steamships operate.

Earth's most important environments. It needs to be preserved if we are to keep these animals alive.

Machu Picchu in Peru is one of the lost cities of the Incas. It is located on a mountainside 7,800 feet above sea level.

Atacama Desert in northern Chile is the driest desert in the world. It has not rained in some parts of this desert in more than 400 years.

Major Cities

Rio de Janeiro, Brazil

Buenos Aires, Argentina

Montevideo, Uruguay

Caracas, Venezuela

Lima, Peru

SPEAK UP!

During my travels, I've learned about many different languages and customs. I have even figured out how to say some phrases in nine different languages (including English). I've outlined some countries below. See if you can match each language with a country where it would be spoken by a majority of the people. The words in parentheses show how to pronounce each phrase in its native language.

HELLO (GOOD DAY)	GOOD-BYE
1. Bon jour (Bon Zhoor)	Au revoir (O reh-vwar)
2. Guten tag (Gooten Tag)	Auf weidersehen (Ouf vee-der-zane)
3. Bon giorno (Bon Zhor-no)	Addio (Ah-dee-oh)
4. Buenos dias (Bway-nose dee-ahs)	Adios (Ah-dee-os)
5. Ohio (O-hi-o)	Sayonara (Sigh-ya-nah-rah)
6. Nihow (Knee-how)	Tzay-jiann (Zeye-jin)
7. Shalom (Shah-loam)	Lihitraot (Le-hit-rah-oat)
8. Strasvitziya (Strass-vee-si-yah)	Dosvidanya (Dose-vee-don-ya)

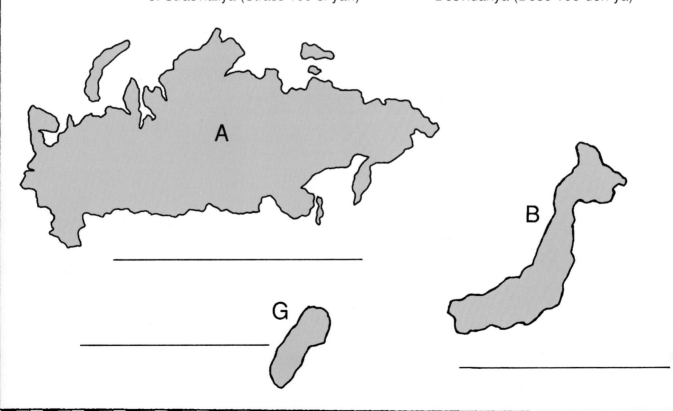

A

G

B

_____

_____

_____

WHICH ONE IS IT?

8. There are two neighboring Middle Eastern countries whose names are spelled exactly the same except for one letter. Which two countries are they?

WHICH ONE IS IT?

9. Excluding Antarctica, only one continent is made up of just one country. Which continent is it?

THANK YOU	LANGUAGE
Merci (Mare-sea)	French
Danke (Donk-ah)	German
Grazie (Graht-see)	Italian
Gracias (Grah-see-ahs)	Spanish
Kansha suru (Can-sha sue-rue)	Japanese
Shieh-shieh (She-a she-a)	Chinese
Todah (Toe-dah)	Hebrew
Spacebo (Spa-see-bow)	Russian

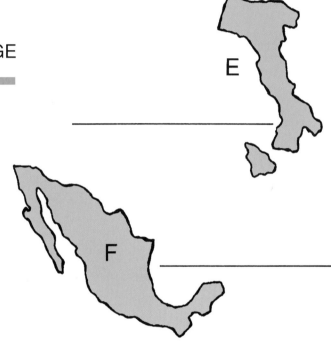

E

_____

F

_____

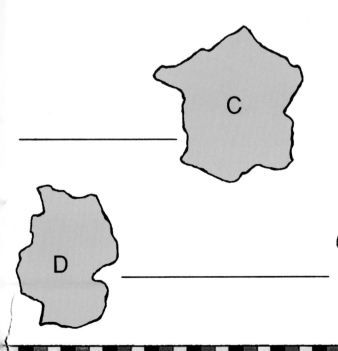

C

_____

D

_____

_____

H

A·N·S·W·E·R·S

For each question, I've given one correct answer. You may sometimes find another answer that fits as well.

NAME GAME (page 6)
Ada - Canada
Al - Mali
Ana - Botswana
Ari - Bulgaria
Ben - Benin
Chad - Chad
Dominic - Dominican Republic
Don - Indonesia
Fran - France
Gary - Hungary
Geri - Nigeria
Guy - Guyana
Ira - Iran
Ken - Kenya
Leon - Sierra Leone
Liz - Belize
Mal - Malawi
Mark - Denmark
Philip - Philippines
Sal - El Salvador
Stan - Afghanistan
Trini - Trinidad and Tobago

CAPITAL LETTERS (page 7)
Tokyo, Japan
Bucharest, Romania
Lagos, Nigeria
Yangon, Myanmar
Jerusalem, Israel
London, England
Canberra, Australia
Montevideo, Uruguay
Taipei, Taiwan
Hanoi, Vietnam

If you've chosen the correct letters the final country was YUGOSLAVIA.

PICTURE PERFECT (pages 10-11)
1. Australia
2. Canada
3. United States
4. France
5. Mexico
6. Kenya
7. Russia

BOTTOM TO TOP (page 14)
Copenhagen, Denmark
Katmandu, Nepal
Buenos Aires, Argentina
Tripoli, Libya
Wellington, New Zealand
Rome, Italy
Paris, France
The pictured country is Finland.

FLAG FUN (page 15)
Spain
New Zealand
Mexico
Argentina
Algeria
Norway
Nigeria
Mozambique

When you unscramble the boxed letters, you'll find that Libya is the only country whose flag is made up of only one color. That color is green.

THE BIGGEST AND BEST
(page 18)
1. Mount Everest is 29,028 feet above sea level.
2. The Nile is 4,160 miles long.
3. Canada measures 3,849,000 square miles.
4. China has a population of more than 1,130,065,000.
5. The Andes run for more than 4,000 miles.
6. The Pacific Ocean measures 64,186,300 square miles.
7. The Sahara measures 3,500,000 square miles.
8. Angel Falls is 3,212 feet high.
9. The Dead Sea in Israel is 1,312 feet below sea level.
10. Lake Superior is 31,700 square miles.

WHAT WAS THAT NAME AGAIN?
(page 19)
1. France
2. Thailand
3. Belize
4. Iran
5. Haiti and the Dominican Republic
6. Zimbabwe
7. Iraq
8. Zaire
9. Taiwan

ENDANGERED ANIMALS
(page 22)
Kenya - Grevy's Zebra
India - Tiger
Tanzania - Black Rhinoceros
Brazil - Giant River Otter
Zaire - Mountain Gorilla
Nepal - Snow Leopard
China - Giant Panda
Australia - Bridled Wallaby

NPVOUBJOT (page 23)
1. McKinley in Alaska
2. Everest in Tibet
3. Kilimanjaro in Tanzania
4. Fuji in Japan
5. Matterhorn in Switzerland
6. Mauna Loa in Hawaii
7. Mont Blanc in France
8. Aconcagua in Argentina
9. Illimani in Bolivia

WHERE ARE THEY? (page 26)
Why do I never go hungry when I'm travelling through the desert? Because of the sand which is there. (sandwiches)

ISLAND HOPPING (page 27)
1. Iceland
2. Madagascar
3. Cuba
4. Japan
5. Sri Lanka
6. Australia

SPEAK UP (pages 30-31)
A - 8 Russia   E - 3 Italy
B - 5 Japan   F - 4 Mexico
C - 1 France   G - 7 Israel
D - 2 Germany   H - 6 China

WHICH ONE IS IT? (various)
1. Greenland
2. Russia
3. Iceland and Ireland
4. X
5. The Great Wall of China
6. Ecuador
7. Oslo, the capital of Norway can be found in Czechoslovakia
8. Iran and Iraq
9. Australia

DATE DUE

PRINTED IN U.S.A

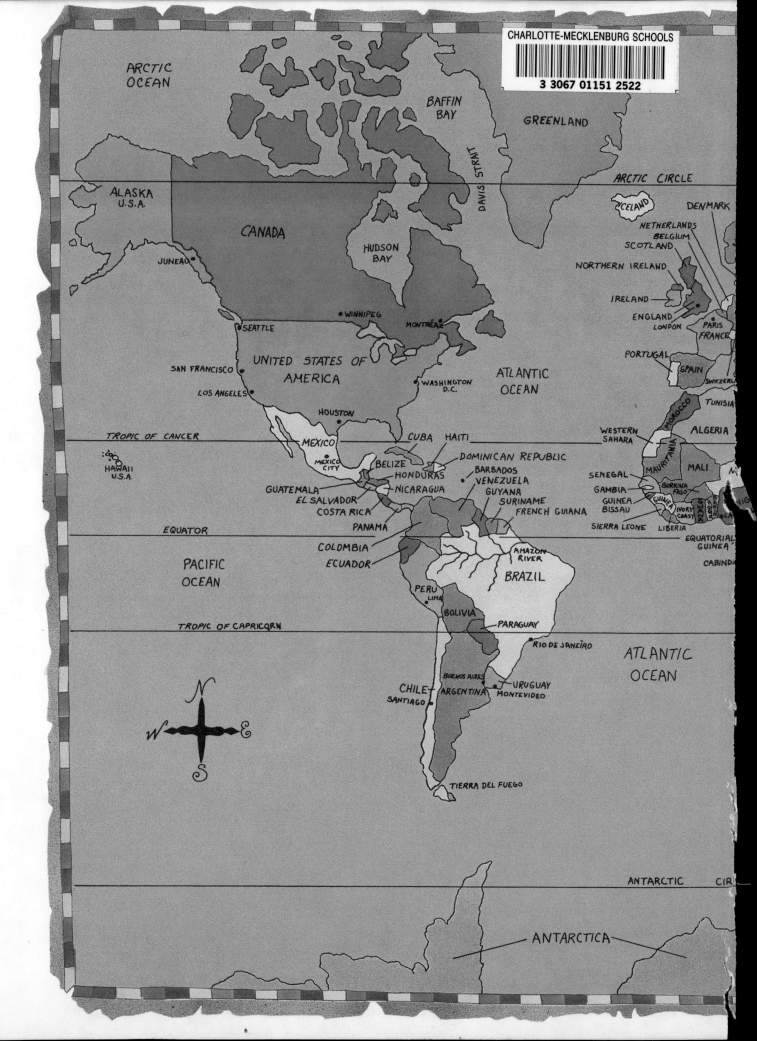